MARGRET & H.A.REY'S
Curious George
and the Birthday Surprise

Illustrated in the style of H. A. Rey by Martha Weston

Houghton Mifflin Company   Boston

www.hmhbooks.com

The text of this book is set in 17-point Adobe Garamond.
The illustrations are watercolor and charcoal pencil, reproduced in full color.

Library of Congress Cataloging-in-Publication data is available for this title.
ISBN 0-618-34688-0 (hardcover)
ISBN 0-618-34687-2 (paperback)

Manufactured in China
SCP   20 19 18 17
4500464661

This is George. He was a good little monkey and always very curious.
"Today is a special day," the man with the yellow hat told George at
breakfast. "I have a surprise planned and lots to do to get ready. You can
help me by staying out of trouble."

George was happy to help.

Later, while George was looking out the window (and being very good), he heard some tinkly music. It was coming from an ice cream truck! George watched as a whole line of children and their dogs enjoyed some ice cream treats. It looked like fun.

But when the ice cream truck moved on, George forgot all about
staying out of trouble and went to find some fun of his own.

In the living room George found noisemakers . . .

and hats . . .

and games!

Could this be part of his friend's surprise?

Before George could find out, he spotted some streamers, balloons, and colored tissue. He could not resist. . . .

7

Decorating was easy
for a little monkey!

PARTY
HATS

Still, George was curious about the surprise. And what was that good smell coming from the kitchen? George followed his nose.

Mmmm. It was a cake! And it looked as good as it smelled. All it needed was frosting. George had seen his friend make frosting before.

But today his friend was busy.
Maybe George could help.
He could frost the cake himself!

First George put a bit of this in the mixing bowl.
Next he added a bit of that.
Then he turned the mixer on.

The frosting whirled
around and around.

It was whirling too fast! But when George tried to stop the mixer it only went faster

and faster

and FASTER!

12

George lifted the beaters out of the bowl. Frosting flew everywhere!

Poor George. He did not mean to make such a mess. He had only wanted to help. Now how could he clean up the sticky kitchen?

Just then George heard the tinkly music again. The ice cream truck was coming back up the street, and George had an idea. Quickly he opened the door . . .

and invited all of the dogs in for a treat!

In no time, the
kitchen was as clean
as a whistle.

When the dogs finished their snack George took them back outside. The ice cream truck was still there. And so was his friend!

"George!" said the man with the yellow hat. "I've been looking for you. It's time for the surprise!"

George had found hats, games, decorations, and a cake.

He was curious.

Was the surprise a party?

Yes! It was a party!
George was happy to see all of his friends.
They were glad to see George, too.
"What great decorations," Bill said.
"What a lot of presents!" said Betsy.

"Why don't you play some games
with the guests, George?" the man
with the yellow hat suggested.
"I have one more thing to do."

When George's friend came back he was carrying a cake covered in candles. This wasn't just any party. It was a birthday party! But George was *still* curious. Whose birthday was it? He watched to see who would blow out the candles.

The man with the yellow hat put the cake down right in front of
George. *That* was a surprise! It was *George's* birthday. The party was
for him!

Everyone sang "Happy Birthday."

Then George took a deep breath . . .

and made a wish.

"Happy Birthday, George!"